Poppy's Purpose

~ based on the true story of a PATH train car ~

written and illustrated by Marie Betts Bartlett

G. Boreas Publishing

Poppy was a passenger railcar who loved what she did every day. She and her sister railcars joined together to form one long train for the PATH railroad that ran between the small cities of New Jersey and the towering skyscrapers of New York City. Back and forth they ran, above the ground, under the ground and even under the Hudson River.

In the mornings, Poppy and her sisters carried thousands of passengers into the big, busy city so that they could go to work. Bankers and builders, dishwashers and doctors, cooks and cashiers. All these people and so many more rode every day on Poppy's train.

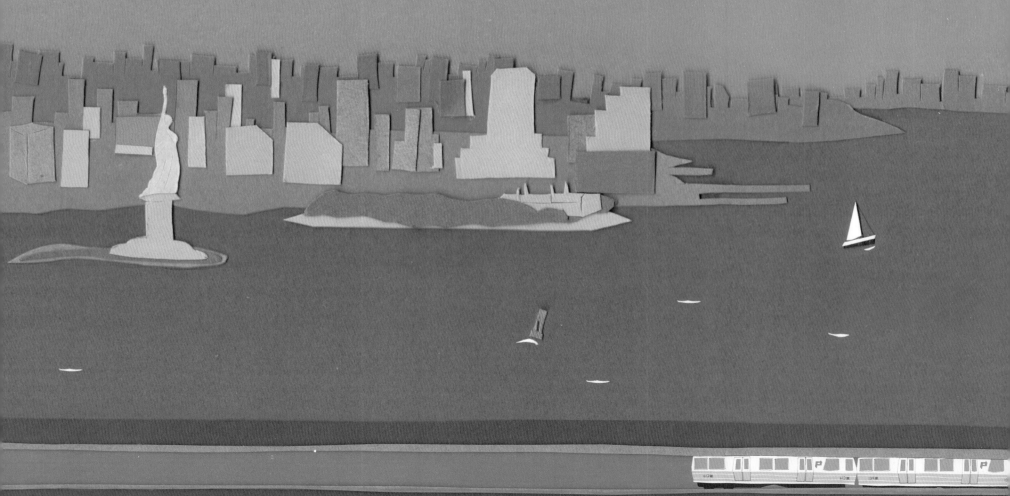

In the evenings, Poppy and her sisters brought the people back beneath the running river, safe and speeding through the underground tunnels. After a long day at work, the weary travellers headed home- home to their families, home to dinner around the table, home to bedtime stories, and home to sleep.

Poppy enjoyed her life because she and her sister railcars moved as a team, and all the people she carried felt like family. When Poppy opened her doors, she welcomed everyone into her car. When the people walked out her sliding doors, she silently wished them a happy day.

One fall morning, Poppy's travels began as usual. The bankers and builders, dishwashers and doctors, cooks and cashiers, and so many other people loaded into her car. They talked quietly, read their newspapers, or listened to music on their headphones. Poppy brought them to the big, busy city and all the people left her car, heading for work and thinking about the day to come.

Poppy rested at her platform in the big city station beneath two tall, tall towers. She was waiting to return to the small cities of New Jersey and pick up more passengers bound for the big, busy city.

But the rest of the day did not happen as anyone expected.

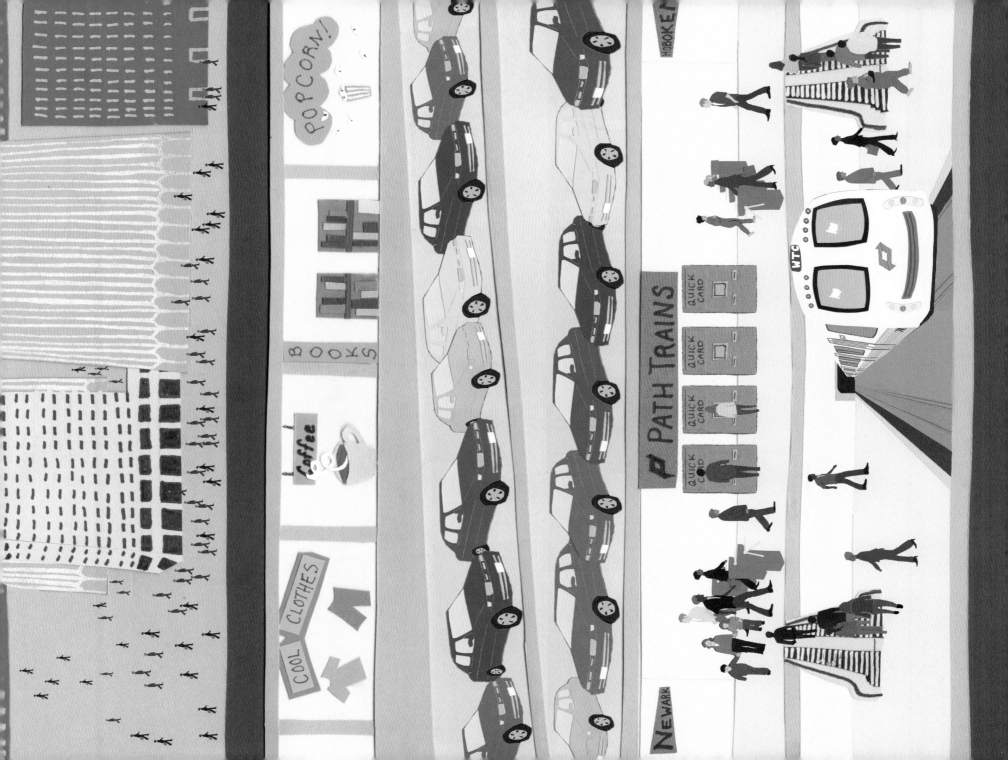

Fire! Fiery flames in the two tall, tall towers!

Poppy heard people shouting and running. They ran out of the underground station or hurriedly left on a train leaving the big city. Poppy wanted to move people too, but she had nobody to run her! Her operator had joined all the other people and escaped from the station.

Poppy had to stay inside her underground station, looking out at the empty platforms. She could only listen to the distant sounds of rescuers helping guide other people to safety.

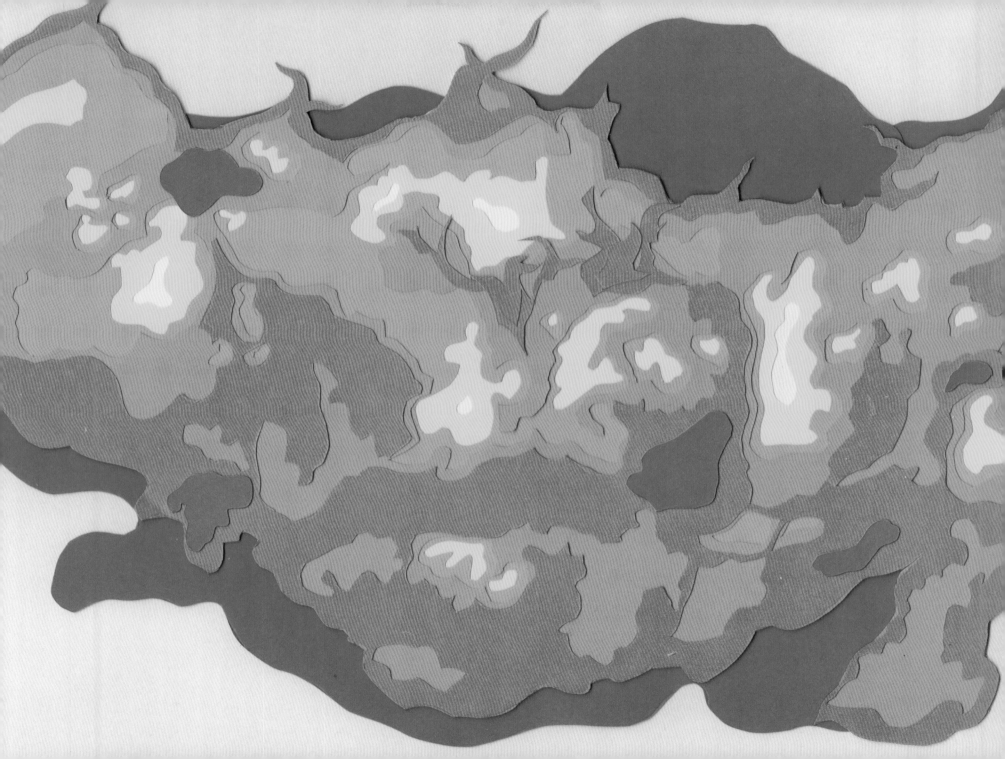

The fires kept burning in the two tall, tall towers. Suddenly, the blazing heat was too much for the skyscrapers. The tall, tall towers tumbled to the ground. Down to the ground they fell, down on top of Poppy's underground train station.

All the lights went out. Darkness and broken building parts surrounded Poppy. But she was safe, safe inside her station, which was so strong and sturdy. The walls and ceilings had protected her from all the falling rubble.

Above the station, the broken buildings had fallen into massive mountains of rubble. Fires still burned deep under the ruins of the towers. Smoke and ashes filled the air. Firefighters hurried to spray water from their hoses onto the sooty, smoky fires.

At first the water just touched
    the rails under Poppy's wheels. More
        water dripped down to Poppy, and the puddle grew
    deeper and deeper. It came up to her wheels. It covered
her motors and crept toward the floor of her car.

Poppy
stayed alone in
the darkness. She
listened to the faraway
sounds of big machinery and
teams of people fighting fires
and cleaning up the piles of broken
buildings.   Poppy didn't know if she
would ever see people again or if she'd ever
be able to move them back and forth from the
little cities of New Jersey to big, busy New York City.
Still, she knew she would be ready if they needed her.

One morning, as Poppy sat silently in her dark, smoky station, she heard quiet voices and a gentle, rhythmic slap, slap on the water. People!!! A small raft holding engineers and rescue people came paddling up the muddy water. They stepped out onto the platform next to Poppy, and one man climbed aboard her! Poppy was overjoyed!

The man shined his flashlight all over Poppy's walls and windows, seats and signal controls. He saw that she had survived the fire and the tumbling towers! Even though she sat in a muddy bath and was dusty and dirty in all the places where she wasn't wet, Poppy had no big dents or dings, scrapes or scratches.

The man wanted to rescue her from under the mountains of rubble and bring her to safety. He said to her, "I can't get you out right now, but I know you are here and I'll be back!" And then he waved goodbye to her, climbed back on the raft with the other people and paddled away.

Poppy wished the man could get her out right then! She wanted to carry passengers, she wanted to be with people, she wanted to be useful! Yet all she could do was wait. And wait. And wait.

Up on top of the mountains of rubble, the firefighters finally were able to put out the sooty, smoky fires, and they turned off their hoses. Water stopped dripping into Poppy's underground station and gradually her muddy bath water drained away.

Months passed, and fall turned into winter. Still the people and machines kept working. Piece by piece the humongous heap of broken buildings grew smaller and smaller. Poppy heard the sounds of all this clean up work, and they seemed to be moving closer and closer to her. But she didn't know if that meant she'd be rescued soon. So she continued to sit, wondering whether the man from the raft would ever return.

And then one cold frosty morning, the man came back! By now, most of the rubble had been cleared away from around Poppy, but getting free still wasn't going to be easy.

Poppy couldn't roll down her track to the outside because the track in front of her was bashed and broken from when the buildings had fallen on it. Plus, Poppy's station had been deep underground. Even though she was almost outside, she was also at the bottom of a huge hole in the ground!

The man and other workers built new track just for rescuing Poppy. Their enormous excavator pulled her along this new track, out of the tunnel and into a bright winter day. Then a colossal crane with a huge pair of slings picked her up, up, up into the air. For a short time, Poppy was flying! The crane swung her onto a nearby tractor trailer that at last, drove her out of the enormous hole.

"Hurray!" Poppy thought. "Now I can carry bankers and builders, dishwashers and doctors, cooks and cashiers and so many more people back and forth between the little cities of New Jersey and big, busy New York City!"

But that did not happen.

Poppy's motors had rusted so much from her muddy bath that they could not be fixed. No more carrying passengers, no more racing down the track under the river, no more travelling back and forth between the cities for Poppy. Instead she was driven to an enormous warehouse where she was parked next to broken building parts, a wrecked sculpture, a damaged firetruck, signs, computers, loads of papers and lots of other things. Everything had been saved from the big fiery fire and the tumbled towers.

Poppy sat there as the seasons changed year after year. After a long while, many of the other stored things were moved out. Not Poppy. She stayed and stayed, wondering again and again if she would ever get to welcome people into her railcar. All she could do was hope. And wait. And hope.

At last, one summer morning the big warehouse doors opened and workers arrived with a tractor trailer. They were taking Poppy to a rail museum! She would get to be with people again!

When Poppy arrived at the museum, she saw a parade with bagpipers and marching rescuers. People clapped and smiled. Poppy looked out at the great crowd that had gathered and was puzzled. She felt happy and excited to be with the people, but they seemed to be celebrating her. She did not know why.

Poppy saw the bankers and builders, dishwashers and doctors, cooks and cashiers, and so many other people, just as she had many years before. But this time she also saw the man from the raft, and the other workers who had helped rescue her from beneath the broken buildings. She saw firefighters, police, ironworkers and more rescuers who had helped people escape from the tall, tall towers. They were all there.

And one by one they came up to Poppy. They sat in her seats, held on to her poles, touched the walls of her car, and they remembered. They remembered what they were doing on the day the towers tumbled, and they remembered the tremendous courage and kindness that so many people showed for others.

A firefighter eased himself into a seat and spoke in a deep, husky voice. "Firefighters from all over came to help get people out of the towers, fight the fires, clean up the broken buildings. So did police, medical people, construction crews- all sorts of people pitched in. They didn't worry about danger, or being hungry or tired. They just wanted to do one thing- to help."

One woman leaned against one of Poppy's poles, closed her eyes, and said, "I was outside and I couldn't see! The air was filled with smoke and dust and I didn't know where to go or what to do. But someone grabbed my arm and helped me walk to safety."

A college student traced his fingers back and forth along the edge of a seat and said, "I was just a little kid back then. But I remember my mom said to me, "I don't know how to put out fires or dig through rubble, but I know those rescuers have to eat. And they're sleeping on sidewalks so they can get right back to work! I'll bring them food and water and blankets. I'll get my friends to help too."

Poppy heard all these stories, and many more. She was startled to realize something new. She might not be moving people back and forth from the small cities of New Jersey to the towering skyscrapers of New York City anymore, but people were celebrating her because Poppy still had an important job to do.

Poppy listened. She gave people a place to come and remember how courage and kindness are always possible. Tall, tall buildings had fallen down on Poppy. But she had survived, and she had been rescued by people who cared. And many other people had also been rescued by brave people who cared, and who put their caring into action.

The force of the fire and the tumbling of the towers reminded everyone that goodness, thoughtfulness and helpfulness always matter. Even people who were usually busy thinking their private thoughts had asked one another, "How are you?" They had reached out to help their neighbors in little ways and big ways. At the museum all these years later, Poppy helped people remember that even in the midst of really, really hard times, they can find goodness.

For so long, Poppy had loved moving people back and forth between the small cities of New Jersey and big busy New York City. At every stop she had opened and closed her doors for them. Now sitting at the museum, Poppy stays in one place. But she still loves what she does. Her doors are always open, and just as she always has, she welcomes everyone into her railcar. She listens to their stories, and gives them a place to sit and to think. And when the people walk out her doors, she silently wishes them a happy day- and a day graced by courage and kindness.

This book is based on the true story of PATH car No. 745. She is on permanent display at Shore Line Trolley Museum in East Haven, CT, waiting to welcome you into her railcar.

Many people and organizations have given me information, images and other support that were essential to the creation of this book. In particular, I am immensely grateful to Wayne Sandford and the Shore Line Trolley Museum; Peter Rinaldi, retired Port Authority engineer; and J.P. Kennedy, Firefighter & Paramedic of Amherst, MA Fire Department and Whately, MA Fire Department. My family and friends have been steady sources of encouragement, advice, artistic and editorial suggestions. My deep thanks to all of you.

- Marie Betts Bartlett